W9-BRX-132

THE FORCE AWAKENS

BY ELIZABETH SCHAEFER   ILLUSTRATED BY DAVID WHITE

ISBN 978-0-545-94072-6

10 9 8 7 6 5 4 3 2 1   16 17 18 19 20

PRINTED IN U.S.A.   40

FIRST PRINTING 2016

BOOK DESIGN BY ERIN MCMAHON

SCHOLASTIC INC.

CHANCE TO **WIN**

GO TO LEGO.COM/LIFESTYLE/FEEDBACK TO FILL OUT A SHORT SURVEY FOR THIS PRODUCT FOR A CHANCE TO WIN A COOL LEGO® SET.*

LEGO.com/lifestyle/feedback

REY AND FINN ACCIDENTALLY RELEASE DANGEROUS CREATURES FROM HAN'S CARGO HOLD THAT DISTRACT THE GANGS.
BUT I'M TOO PRETTY TO GET EATEN!

WITH THE GANGS OUT OF THE WAY, HAN TAKES EVERYONE TO MEET HIS OLD FRIEND MAZ. SHE OWNS A BIG CASTLE WHERE ALIENS FROM ALL OVER THE GALAXY COME TO HAVE FUN.

AT LEAST THERE'S NO SAND IN MY FOOD!

MAZ USED TO KNOW LUKE SKYWALKER, AND HAS BEEN KEEPING HIS OLD LIGHTSABER SAFE. REY DOESN'T WANT IT, SO SHE GIVES IT TO FINN.

FINN GETS THE CHANCE TO TRY THE NEW WEAPON SOONER THAN HE WOULD LIKE! THE FIRST ORDER TRACKS THE *MILLENNIUM FALCON* TO MAZ'S CASTLE AND ATTACKS.

FINN, BB-8, HAN, AND CHEWIE FLY TO THE
RESISTANCE HEADQUARTERS. THERE THEY MEET
GENERAL LEIA ORGANA—THE LEADER OF THE
RESISTANCE. TOGETHER THEY COME UP WITH A
PLAN TO DESTROY THE FIRST ORDER BASE AND
RESCUE REY.

I TRIED CALLING.
I SWEAR!